THE BUTTERFLY PRINCESS
RAINBOW SEED

Tenzin Choekyi

AuthorHouse™ UK
1663 Liberty Drive
Bloomington, IN 47403 USA
www.authorhouse.co.uk
Phone: 0800.197.4150

Published by AuthorHouse 03/29/2019

ISBN: 978-1-7283-8681-2 (sc)
ISBN: 978-1-7283-8680-5 (e)

authorHOUSE®

TABLE OF CONTENTS

CHAPTER 1
THE SEED

Once upon a time, a boy walked down to the
ordinary Lily Lotus Flower Park.

Suddenly, a shining light-brown seed fell out of the boy's pocket.

The seed softly fell on the ground and burrowed into the soil.

Inside the soil, the seed found its comfort and soft zone. And the seed happily slept in the soil.

CHAPTER 2
THE SEED GROWS

While the Glitter Princess Rainbow Seed was sleeping in the cosy, soft soil, something made her awaken. It was the sounds of children playing, cheering, and dancing.

Then, its big, brown left eye and long black eyelashes opened with a pop sound. The right eye opened with a pop sound too. A few moments later, a tiny nose gradually came out. And she giggled and smiled joyfully.

The shining round seed heard the children going, "Ahahahahah." She really wanted to go outside, but she had no hands. So she tried to stretch her head to see what was going on. And she stretched slowly again and again. All of sudden, legs popped out, and they started growing a little bigger and longer.

Then a miracle happened to her. A magical rain came down hard, and thunder sounded. She began to drink the magic rain.

After a while, she grew two petals of her hair up through the ground.

CHAPTER 3
THE MAGIC RAINBOW

When the rain stopped, a rainbow appeared in the sky. The end of the rainbow appeared on Glitter Princess Rainbow Seed's head. But the rainbow wasn't any old rainbow. It was magical. While the rainbow was there, Glitter Princess Rainbow Seed's leaves grew taller and started changing colours. They were red, orange, yellow, and green. She began to smile happily.

She grew bigger and bigger. And she began to make friends with some insects, like the worm Dhawa dolma, the ant Rhasa, and the Mr millipede.

She asked, "What does it look like outside?"

"Children are playing happily outside," replied Rhasa.

"It is very hot for me. I like staying underground," said Dhawa Dolma.

Mr millipede added, "I can have some yummy leaves to crunch there."

CHAPTER 4
THE SILVER WORLD

When the rainbow had gone, the Glitter Princess Rainbow Seed gradually cracked the soil and grew on the ground until she was fully above ground—well, except for her roots. The clear, brilliant moonlight was like a silver world. She was amazed and said, "Wow!"

She looked up and saw beautiful shining stars, twinkling and happily waving to the Glitter Princess Rainbow Seed from the sky. Then a magnificent and mellow-moon lady came and said, "Welcome to the silver world."

Glitter Seed Princess Rainbow Seed beamed on and stretched herself. She breathed some the fresh air and smelled the fragrances of flowers and plants. She could hear a musical sound of owls hooting. The frog said, "Bobbed, bobbed, bobbed, bobbed." And the bugs went, "Sk, sk, sk, sk," as they crept around.

CHAPTER 5
THE SUNNY MORNING

It was warm and bright when Glitter Princess Rainbow Seed woke up. She stretched again, and when her eyes were finally open, she saw a giant smile from the sun. With a gentle voice, the sun said, "You are so cute and gorgeous."

"Thank you," replied Glitter Princess Rainbow Seed.

Then she looked around and saw a lot of flowers. She saw blue nigellas, pink cosmos, and red roses among the flowers. But Glitter Princess Rainbow Seed only had rainbow petals. Many creatures came to say, "Good morning," to her. They included a yellow-and-black striped busy bee, a colourful butterfly, and a red ladybird with black dots.

Then the wind started blowing slightly. The wind stroked her face gently, and the whole wild world started dancing happily to the rustling music. The Glitter Princess Rainbow Seed also danced joyfully until the sun waved goodbye to her. The Glitter Princess Rainbow Seed was really pleased that everyone was so welcoming to her.

CHAPTER 6
THE TRANSFORMER

The Glitter Princess Rainbow Seed saw something from far away. It was a playground, where children were playing gleefully. She wished that she could also play with those children.

All of sudden, she called out, "Crystal alive." Then she gradually transformed into a human girl! She slowly grew long, straight, shiny human rainbow hair. It grew longer and longer, until it touched the ground.

Glitter Princess Rainbow Seed's eyes grew big and brown. She had rainbow eyelashes, and her face white with peach cheeks. Her lips were red. And her teeth were as white as the moonlight.

Then fingers popped out on both her hands. Her fingernails were shining and glittering.

She had rainbow earrings, and a rainbow diamond necklace was on her chest. The yellow dress with rainbow dots looked perfect on her.

A pair of beautiful brown, glittering, knee-length boots with long strings were tied around her green leggings.

CHAPTER 7
LEENA

Every step she took on the grass turned into silver, glittering footprints. A few seconds later, the ground absorbed them into the soil.

Glitter Princess Rainbow Seed ran to the playground and played with all the children. "My name is Leena. What is your name?" she asked a little girl. The little girl was deaf and shook her head. "Come on, give me a high-five," Leena said. They gave each other a high-five, and Leena started off to play with other children.

Then the most amazing thing happened. The little girl could talk. "Mummy, Mummy, I can talk now," she cried.

Leena said, "Go back now." She waved goodbye to her. Then she happily turned back into a flower.

CHAPTER 8
AUTUMN

Glitter Princess Rainbow Seed said, "It's time to change clothes." So the flowers, plants, and trees started gradually turning into brown leaves and fell on the ground. But not all the leaves were brown. Some were red, yellow, gold, and silver. The gold ones were as gold as the sun. The world was colourful and beautiful.

Meanwhile, Glitter Princess Rainbow Seed saw a group of children grouped in twos. They were collecting leaves and sticks to make a house with windows.

She wanted to play, so she again said, "Crystal alive." And again, she transformed into a human. But this time, someone spotted her.

Luckily, she said, "Invisibility go," and quick as a flash, she became invisible. She picked a bunch of leaves and dropped them on the ground. Then she jumped up and down in the bunch of leaves. After that, she said, "Earring glow." Her earring began to glow, and she turned into a flower again.

CHAPTER 9
SNOW TIME

"Oh, no. It's time to change our clothes again," complained Glitter Princess Rainbow Seed. So all the creatures started wear white clothes. The time had arrived for creatures and Glitter Princess Rainbow Seed to celebrate the beautiful winter.

Glittering Princess Rainbow Seed said, "Crystal alive," and was transformed into a snow princess. She wore a shiny diamond crown on her rainbow hair. She wore a sparkling snow dress, a bit like Elsa's dress in the movie Frozen.

As Leena walked, all her silver, glittering footprints dissolved into the snow. When she saw some dust on the ground, she built a snow queen on the top of it.

Suddenly, the snow queen became alive. She told Leena, "Thank you for making me." They held hands and played together. They even tried catching snowflakes on their tongues.

After a while, the winter celebration party really started. All the creatures dressed up in their best clothes. The best thing about the party was that they had a snow cake. They also sang and danced in the snowflake drops. Moreover, they made different types of animal footprints. And then the arts of winter closed.

I will see you in my next book.

Watch out for The Flower Girl.